CONTENTS

Welcome To Toyland 6

Picture Stories
Noddy's Silly Mistake 12
Noddy Flies A Kite 18
Noddy's Clever Car 30
Goodwill To All Toyland 34
Noddy And The Pile Of Snow 46
Noddy's Lost Basket 72
A Bag Of Mixed Spells 76
Mrs. Noah Gets A Shock 88
Good Old Big-Ears 94
Noddy And The Wooden Horse 106

Bedtime Stories
The Lost Key 52
Noddy And The Moon 60

Little Rhymes
Hello 10
Toy Town Market 16
Hold On To Your Hat! 28

Noddy's Passengers 33
Father Christmas 45
Snow Stars 48
Can I Have A Story, Please? 50
Sleepy Time 66
A Naughty Breeze 69
Bumpy's Bathtime 75
Vanishing Act 85
What's That Noise? 91

Toyland Puzzles and Games
Special Deliveries 11
To Market, To Market 14
'M' For Market 17
Kites In The Park 26
Hats Away! 29
Road Block 32
Noddy's Christmas Counting 42
A Silly Stocking 44
A Special Snowflake 49
Sky High 67
What's The Story? 68
Where Are Noddy's Cakes? 70
Which Way To Noddy's House? 74
Noddy The Wizard 84
A Walk Through Magic Village 86
Spots And Stripes 90
Hello, Mrs. Noah 92
Who Goes There? 102
A Woodland Walk 104
A Tow Back To Toy Town 108

NODDY

ANNUAL 2003

Pedigree®

Published by Pedigree Books Limited
The Old Rectory, Matford Lane, Exeter, EX2 4PS.
E-mail books@pedigreegroup.co.uk
Published 2002

£6.99

WELCOME TO TOYLAND

HELLO, EVERYONE!

My name is Noddy and I live in a special part of Toyland called Toy Town. What do you think I am doing today? That's right, I'm doing a little shopping in Toy Town market. I'm in a hurry, as I have lots of passengers to take about this afternoon, but I have just enough time to tell you that this year's annual is jam-packed with stories, puzzles, rhymes and games, telling you all about my adventures. Where has Dinah Doll got to? Let's see if we can find her - and some other Toyland friends...

DINAH DOLL

Here is Dinah Doll! Dinah runs my favourite stall in Toy Town market. She always has something that I want to buy and serves me with a friendly smile. She's a very good friend of mine, too!

BIG-EARS

My best friend is Big-Ears the Brownie. He lives in Toadstool Wood and is always there to help if I have any trouble with the naughty goblins. He also makes the best tea and cakes ever!

NODDY'S CAR

When I have finished my shopping, I get back into my little red and yellow taxi. We are always very busy, taking passengers around Toy Town and greeting everyone with a "Parp! Parp!" of the car horn.

TESSIE BEAR

Tessie Bear is another of my good friends. Her dog, Bumpy, is always jumping around and often knocks me right over! Tessie Bear is very kind to me and will always pop in if she's passing.

MR. PLOD

Toy Town's policeman is called Mr. Plod. I'm only ever in trouble with him for driving too fast. He spends most of his time chasing after those mischievous goblins, Sly and Gobbo!

MR. AND MRS. NOAH

In the Toy Town harbour rests Mr. and Mrs. Noah's ark. In their ark live pairs of every animal you can think of! They always have so much to do, but still manage to find time for a trip out now and then.

MISS PINK CAT

My friend Miss Pink Cat loves to wear hats. She once asked me to take her to a hat shop in Magic Village. You can read about what happened when we went there later in this annual!

GOBBO

There are lots of naughty goblins that live in Toyland's Dark Wood and Gobbo is one of them. He and his best friend, Sly, are always playing tricks on me and have stolen my car more than once!

SLY

Sly by name and sly by nature, this mischievous goblin is never far away. I'm very lucky that Big-Ears and Mr. Plod always make sure that Sly and Gobbo pay for the tricks they play on me!

HELLO

Hello, hello, does anybody
Want some help from little Noddy?

Parcels fetched and shopping done,
Letters posted, errands run

Windows cleaned, and doorsteps too
Goods delivered all day through!

If you're wanting cakes for tea
Or eggs for supper, shout for me!

SPECIAL DELIVERIES

Noddy is always happy to help his friends in Toy Town. Today he has fetched some parcels from the station and is going to deliver them. Unjumble the letters to see who each parcel is for. The answers are at the bottom of the page.

Bgi raEs

siTsee eaBr

naDhi loDl

rM rKapsS

11

NODDY'S SILLY MISTAKE

Whilst out shopping one day, Tessie Bear spotted Noddy and called to him.

"I left Bumpy Dog tied up at the market," she explained. "Could you fetch him?"

Noddy always likes to help. He went to the market and found Bumpy Dog.

Noddy untied a rope and walked off with it. It was the wrong rope. Stop, Noddy!

There was a cow on the end of Noddy's rope! Martha Monkey was very puzzled.

The cow lumbered happily after Noddy. "That's not Bumpy Dog!" cried Tessie.

Noddy did get a shock! "Goodness! Bumpy Dog has turned into a cow!" he cried.

Tessie told Noddy to take the cow straight back and get Bumpy. What a silly mistake!

TO MARKET, TO MARKET

Noddy loves going to Toy Town market, especially if he doesn't have to fetch Bumpy Dog! Look at the things below and use a pencil to join up the pairs that are sold on the same stall. Say which stall each of the pairs can be found on as you do them. The answers are at the bottom of the page.

Answers: Sandals and boots are sold on a shoe stall; apples and oranges are on a fruit stall; t-shirts and jumpers are on a clothes stall; balls and skipping ropes are on a toy stall.

TOY TOWN MARKET

Fruit and vegetables, bread and cakes,
Buckets, bowls and garden rakes,
Clothes and shoes, kites and balls
Are sold on Toy Town's market stalls.

So are flowers, cheese and jam,
Beads and bangles, pies and ham,
Noddy loves the market place -
He knows he'll see a friendly face!

'M' IS FOR MARKET

'M' is for market and Martha Monkey. Look at the things that Martha has bought from Toy Town market and colour in all the ones that begin with 'm'.

17

NODDY FLIES A KITE

One morning, Noddy woke up to find the wind blowing in at his windows and making his door rattle. He looked out of his House-For-One. "Good morning, Noddy!" Master Tubby called to him. "Dear me, what a windy day it is!"

"The wind certainly is windy today," agreed Noddy. Master Tubby laughed and walked over. "You know, it's a good day for flying a kite," he said. "I don't have a kite," Noddy told him. "Borrow mine," smiled Master Tubby. "See you after breakfast."

Noddy quickly got dressed and had breakfast, then hurried to Master Tubby's house. What a lovely kite there was waiting for him. "You'll have fun with this," Master Tubby smiled. "Look after it, though - I'm fond of that kite!" "Thank you!" said Noddy.

Noddy was pleased with the kite. He drove out to the Toyland countryside and chose a field to fly it in. Goodness, how it flew! It tugged so hard at the string that Noddy almost let go. "I can't hold you if you tug my fingers like that!" he cried.

"I'll put on my gloves, then I can hold you better," said Noddy. He tied the kite to the back of the car so that he could get his gloves on.

Dear me, the kite started to pull Noddy's car along backwards! "Stop, kite! Stop, car!" Noddy yelled in alarm and began to run. "Stop, I tell you!"

The kite tugged away at the car, bumping it across the field. "Please stop!" Noddy cried, chasing after it. He caught up and jumped on to the bonnet, just as the car was speeding through a gate. How the hens clucked and how the ducks quacked!

Noddy jumped into the car, but the kite was pulling so hard that the brakes would not work! BUMP! The car bounced over a stone. SCRAPE! The kite tugged the car over a prickly hedge. The cow on the other side had quite a surprise!

Noddy tried to steer the car, but it was tricky going backwards so quickly. Bumpity bump over another field went the car. BUMP! It bounced over a bank into a pond. SPLASH! "Oh, no!" cried Noddy. "Now I'm getting wet!"

Oh, dear. What a long way poor Noddy and his car had gone - all backwards, too! Then the wind began to drop, and so did the kite. Noddy watched as it drifted down into a tall tree. "Thank goodness, we're stopping!" he sighed.

"What a journey!" Noddy exclaimed, as he went over to the tree. He peered up into the branches and saw that the kite was stuck fast, near the top.

"Oh, dear!" Noddy said to himself. "The kite is tangled on a high branch. However shall I get it down?" His little bell jingled as he thought about what to do.

Noddy decided he would have to climb the tree. He could not go back without Master Tubby's kite! He clambered up and up through the branches until he could reach the kite and untangle it. Meanwhile, there was someone down below...

Noddy's car heard the goblins coming and hid in a bush. "It's time we taught Big-Ears a lesson," said Sly. "He's always getting Mr. Plod on to us."

Noddy listened as the goblins talked. "I know," said Gobbo. "Let's go and steal his bike. He'll be lost without it!" The goblins cackled and ran off.

Noddy could hardly believe his wooden ears. He slithered down the tree with the kite. His car came out of the bushes and Noddy leapt in. They set off at top speed for Big-Ears' house, to warn him before the goblins got there.

Noddy told Big-Ears what he had heard. "I'll find Mr. Plod and tell him to come straight away," said Big-Ears. "We'll show those goblins!"

Noddy and Big-Ears hid as the goblins approached. Just as Sly started to wheel away Big-Ears' bike, Mr. Plod arrived. "Your bike, is it?" he boomed.

Mr. Plod took the naughty goblins away to the police station for a stern telling off. Noddy got in his car and said goodbye. "Won't you stay for tea?" called Big-Ears. "No, thank you," replied Noddy. "I have a clever kite to take back!"

KITES IN THE PARK

Noddy has gone to the park to fly kites with Big-Ears and Tessie Bear. It's so windy, though, that their kites have all got tangled up! Whose kite is stuck in the tree? Follow the strings to find out, then say whose kite is flying away.

Do you have a kite? What colour is it? Use your pens or crayons to make the kite below into a kite you would like to take to the park. Don't forget to decorate the tail with bows or flowers - or anything else you want!

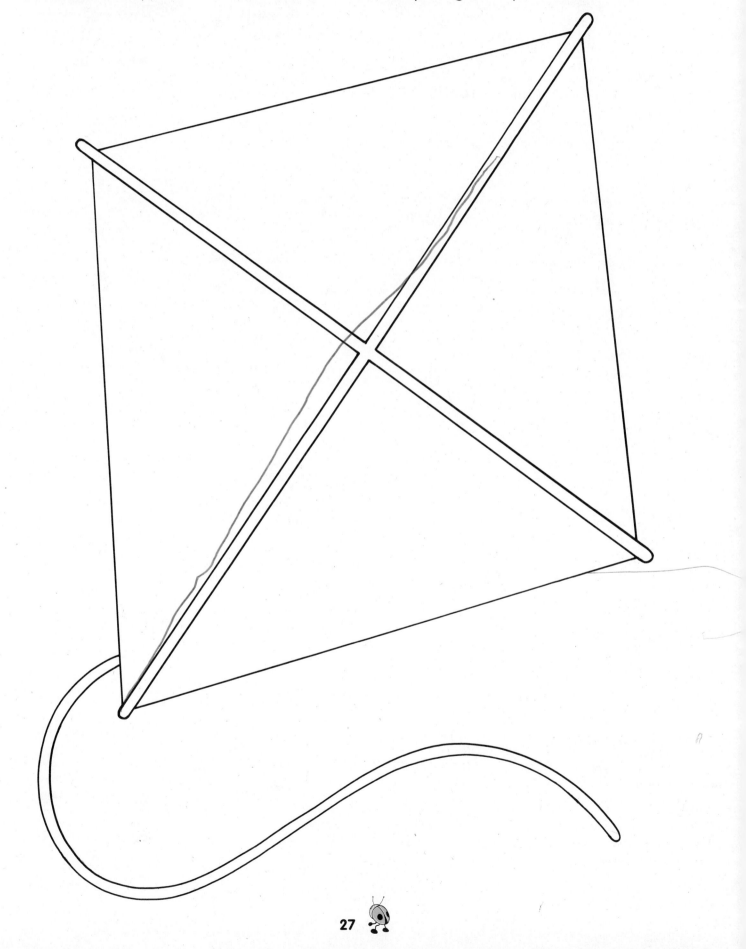

27

HOLD ON TO YOUR HAT

The wind is strong,
The sun is bright,
So Noddy wants
to Fly his kite.

He sends it upwards
And grips the string,
The breeze on his hat
Makes it jingle-jing,

But watch out, Noddy,
It's gusty today,
If you don't hold that hat
It will blow away!

HATS AWAY!

It's been such a windy day that lots of hats have been handed in to Toy Town police station. Help Mr. Plod to return them all by saying whose hat you think each one is. The answers are at the bottom of the page.

1

2

3

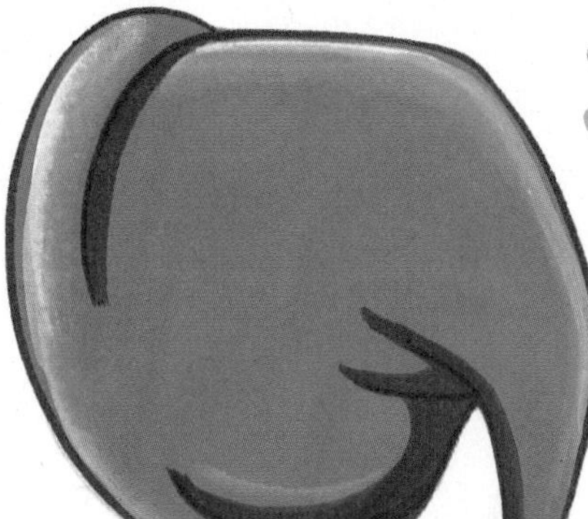

4

5

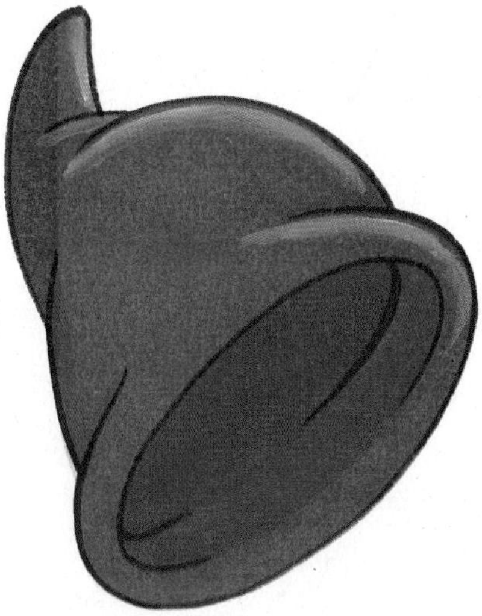

Answers: The hats belong to: 1. Tessie Bear 2. Mr. Wobbly Man 3. Noddy 4. Big-Ears 5. Miss Pink Cat

NODDY'S CLEVER CAR

One afternoon, Noddy's little car stopped for no reason. "Oh, dear," said Noddy.

Noddy looked at his car. "There's nothing wrong," he said. "We must need petrol."

"I'll help you push your car," Sly said. "There's a garage at the bottom of the hill."

"I'll easily push the car down here, Noddy," smiled Sly Goblin. "Here it goes!"

As the car set off, Sly jumped in. "Thanks for the ride, Noddy!" he cackled.

The car raced off down the hill. "Sly's stolen my car!" cried Noddy. "Stop him!"

Sly put some petrol in the car. What do you think the car did when it was full?

It raced straight back to Noddy. "What a clever little car you are!" Noddy cried.

ROAD BLOCK

Something has made Noddy stop his car. He's in a hurry, too!
Join the dots to find out what is blocking the road, then use your
crayons or pens to colour the rest of the picture.

NODDY'S PASSENGERS

Noddy is the happy fellow
Whose little car is red and yellow,
He's taking passengers round Toy Town,
First Dinah Doll, then Clockwork Clown,

Mr. Jumbo, Tessie Bear,
Then Mrs. Skittle and a pair
Of little Skittles, Miss Pink Cat
(Shopping for a nice new hat),

Mrs. Noah and Mr. Plod,
Sammy with his fishing rod,
The Tubby Bears are going away,
Goodness, Noddy's busy today!

GOODWILL TO ALL TOYLAND

It was Christmas Eve and Noddy was spending the morning finishing his Christmas shopping. He had bought so many things, he could hardly carry them all. "I just need to get some chocolates for Big-Ears," he said to himself.

Noddy bought some chocolates, then went home to wrap what he had bought. It took him a long time, but he did not mind. Noddy loved getting ready for Christmas. He hoped that Father Christmas would bring him some nice things.

Noddy had tea and, after a final check that everything was wrapped and labelled, got ready for bed. "I mustn't forget to put my stocking out," he said, hanging his stocking at the end of the bed. "Father Christmas will be looking for it."

Noddy was so excited, it took him a long time to get to sleep. Eventually, his eyes stayed closed and he had dreams about playing in the snow.

When Father Christmas was sure that little Noddy was fast asleep, he crept up to the bed and filled the stocking with lots of lovely presents.

When Noddy awoke, he almost forgot that it was Christmas Day. Suddenly remembering, he jumped up and scrambled to his stocking. "Father Christmas has been!" he exclaimed with delight. "What a lot of presents!"

Noddy was very pleased with his presents. After breakfast, he put all his parcels in the car and set off to deliver them. His first stop would be Big-Ears' house. He did not know he was being watched as he drove through the Dark Wood.

Sly and Gobbo, the naughty goblins, followed Noddy's car to Toadstool Wood. "Look at all those Christmas presents," whispered Sly. "Let's take some when Noddy goes inside," Gobbo nodded. "He won't miss one or two."

Once Noddy had gone in, the goblins trotted to his car. "I'll have this one, I think," said Sly, grabbing a parcel. "And I'll have this one," added Gobbo.

"Come on, then!" said Sly. "Let's go before Noddy comes out and sees us." "Right," agreed Gobbo. "Ready, steady...run for it!"

BUMP! The goblins were not looking where they were going and ran straight into Mr. Plod. "Oops-a-daisy," he boomed. "Lucky I brought Big-Ears' present when I did. I was just in time to see you take those parcels from Noddy's car."

Mr. Plod frowned. "Couldn't you goblins have given it a rest, just for Christmas Day?" The goblins looked down at their feet, ashamed. "Now turn round," Mr. Plod continued, "and ring the doorbell, so you can apologise to Noddy."

Gobbo rang the bell and waited for Big-Ears and Noddy to come to the door. "Good morning," Mr. Plod greeted them. "Season's greetings to you both. I caught these goblins stealing your presents, Noddy. They want to say sorry."

Mr. Plod gave the goblins a nudge. "Sorry, Noddy," they mumbled, but Noddy started to giggle. They wondered why he wasn't cross with them.

"You silly goblins," chuckled Noddy. "Look at the labels!" The goblins took a closer look at the presents. The labels had their names on them!

"You bought presents for the goblins?" asked Big-Ears, surprised. "Yes," smiled Noddy. "It is the season of goodwill." "Well, I never," said Mr. Plod. "The goblins stole their own presents!" Everyone laughed, except the goblins.

Big-Ears looked at the sheepish goblins. "Well, if Noddy's being so kind, I shall, too," he said. "Come and have lunch. There'll be plenty." Mr. Plod and the goblins went into Big-Ears' house. There was a delicious smell of Christmas cooking.

Big-Ears served a delicious Christmas lunch and handed round crackers for everyone. Sly and Gobbo were very happy. "Thank you, Big-Ears," said Sly. "And thank you, Noddy," added Gobbo. "Merry Christmas, everyone!"

NODDY'S CHRISTMAS COUNTING

Noddy loves getting ready for Christmas, don't you? He has been busy doing lots of Christmas shopping at the Toy Town shops. Help him to check he has everything by counting all the Christmas things below and writing the numbers in the boxes.

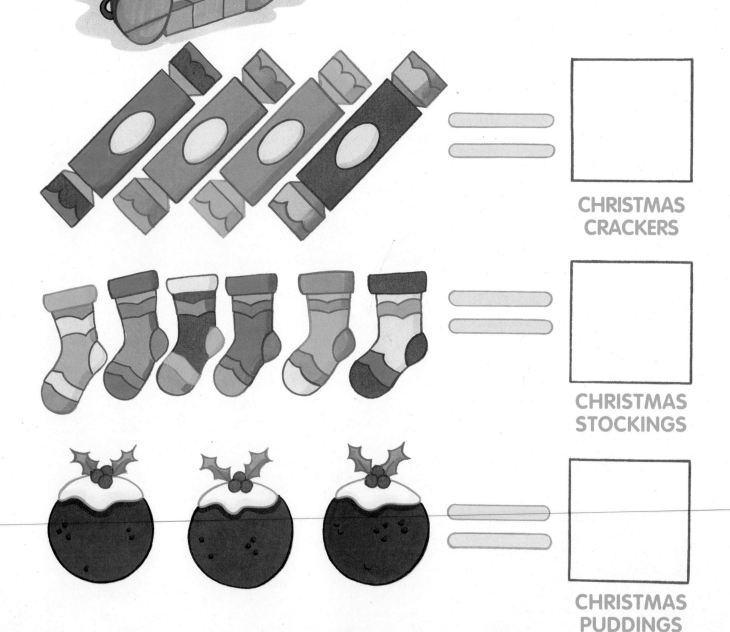

CHRISTMAS CRACKERS

CHRISTMAS STOCKINGS

CHRISTMAS PUDDINGS

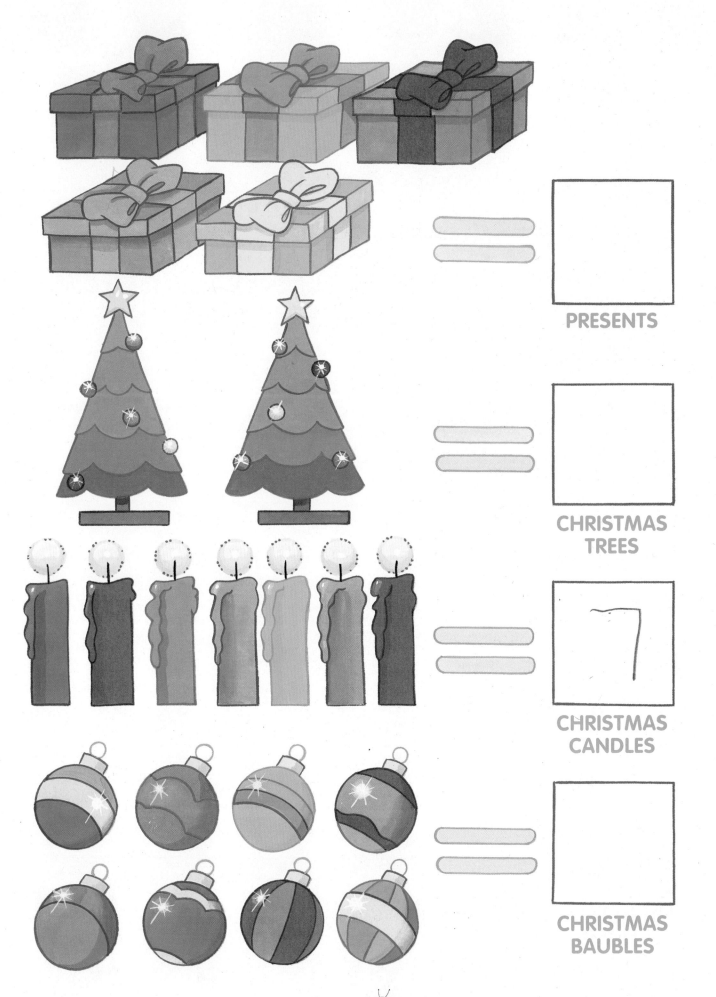

PRESENTS

CHRISTMAS
TREES

CHRISTMAS
CANDLES

CHRISTMAS
BAUBLES

43

A SILLY STOCKING

Join in this Christmas story by saying what the pictures
are as they appear.

One Christmas,  went to stay with . He was

very excited about  coming and put his at the

end of the bed. When he woke up on Christmas morning,

the was empty. " forgot about me!" he sobbed

to . "Oh, ," chuckled . "There's a hole

in your . Your presents are there. Look!" Then

saw lots of parcels on the floor at the end of his bed.

"Oh, thank you, !" he cried.

FATHER CHRISTMAS

His beard is white,
His coat is red,
He creeps in
While you lie in bed.

But close your eyes,
You must not peep!
He'll only come
If you're asleep!

NODDY AND THE PILE OF SNOW

"It's very cold," Noddy said to himself one frosty day. "I think I need a hot drink."

Noddy went into the warm tea shop for tea and cake. He spent all afternoon there.

When Noddy came out, he saw there had been lots of snow. His car was buried!

Noddy's car had so much snow on it, he could not drive it. He had to push it home!

When Noddy went to his garage the next day, all he found was a wet wooden cart!

Noddy told Big-Ears that his car was gone. Big-Ears asked where he had it last.

Big-Ears took Noddy back to the tea shop. Noddy's car was where he had left it!

The pair dragged the cart back. "Whatever will you do next, Noddy?" panted Big-Ears.

SNOW STARS

One day, when it was cold and bright,
Snow came down from above,
And so I held my hand out
To catch some on my glove.

The little flakes were just like stars,
They sparkled in the sun,
I counted all the points they had:
Six on every one!

SPECIAL SNOWFLAKE

When Noddy counted the points on his snowflakes, he found that there were six on each one. Look at the snowflakes below and say which is the odd one out and why. The answer is at the bottom of the page.

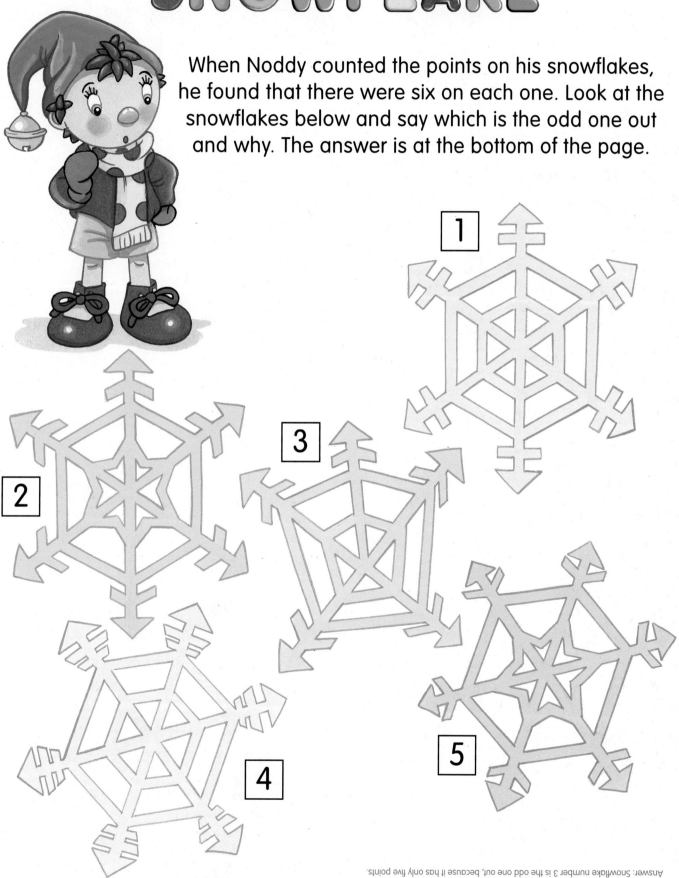

CAN I HAVE A STORY, PLEASE?

Can I have a story
Before I go to bed?
I promise not to say a word
While my story's read.

I'll listen and sit still, I will,
Until the story's done,
And if I'm really, really good...
Can I have another one?

NODDY'S BEDTIME STORIES

The Lost Key
Noddy and the Moon

THE LOST KEY

One morning, Noddy went to see his friend Big-Ears in his house in Toadstool Wood.

"Come in, Noddy," said Big-Ears. "I'm just going to have a cup of tea and a chocolate biscuit. Would you like some?"

"Ooh, yes please," said Noddy, sitting down at the table.

Noddy had just finished his tea and biscuits when there was a knock at the door.

"Is Noddy here?" asked Mrs. Skittle. "I'd like him to take me and my little Skittles to the station, please."

Noddy drove Mrs. Skittle and two of her children to Toy Town station in his little red and yellow taxi. When they arrived, Mrs. Skittle gave Noddy two sixpences: one to pay for herself and one for the little Skittles, who each went for half price. Noddy saw them all off on the Toyland Express. What a crowd there was on the platform! He said hello to Mrs. Tubby Bear, who was waving off Mr. Tubby Bear. Mr. Wobbly Man was there, too, being wobbled about all over the place by the crowd. Noddy had to help him on to the train, since he was wobbling so much he couldn't get on by himself.

Off went the busy Toyland Express, chuff-chuff-chuffing its way towards Rocking Horse Village. Its carriages were full to bursting. Noddy waved till it was out of sight, then went to find some more passengers.

"Parp! Parp!" went his car's horn in the high street. Clockwork Clown waved to him.

"Hey, Noddy!" he called. "Can you take me to my Uncle Click's?"

He jumped into the car and told Noddy that he was late.

"Could you go extra quickly, please, Noddy?" he asked, so Noddy set off at top speed. Along they sped through the Toyland countryside, bumpity-bump! Be careful, Noddy! They came to an extra big bump in the road and the clown nearly shot out of his seat. Neither he nor Noddy noticed that his key flew out of his back on to the road. Oh, dear. He needs that to wind him up when he stops. Wait, Noddy!

When they arrived at
Uncle Click's, Clockwork
Clown stopped at the gate.
"I need winding up," he told Noddy. "Could
you do it for me, Noddy? Use the key in my back."
"But your key's gone!" gasped Noddy. "Where can it be?"
Clockwork Clown was very upset that his key was missing.
"It must have popped out when we went over one of those bumps!" he
exclaimed. "You shouldn't have driven so fast, Noddy!"
"But you asked me to!" Noddy protested. "Let's go
back and look for it," he added, but the clown
could not move until he was wound up again.

Noddy had to go on his own to the place where the car had had a big BUMP, but there was no key there. Noddy called to Mr. Sparks, who was out taking a walk:
"Have you seen a key anywhere around here, Mr. Sparks?"
"Yes, Noddy," Mr. Sparks replied. "Miss Pink Cat picked it up and took it home."
Noddy got back in his car and went to Miss Pink Cat's house to collect the key.

"Oh, dear," said Miss Pink Cat, when Noddy asked for it. "I thought it belonged to Clockwork Mouse. I took it to his house, but he was out, so I left it on his doorstep. I'm very sorry."

Noddy was getting a little cross. He went to Clockwork Mouse's house to see if he was in. "I found the key," Clockwork Mouse told him, "but because it wasn't mine, I left it at the station for the Clockwork Train. I thought the driver must have lost it."
"Bother this key!" frowned Noddy, as he drove to the station. "I've been to the station already today!"
When he got there, the Clockwork Train driver didn't have it either.
"It wasn't for my train," he told Noddy.
"So I handed it in to Mr. Plod. I thought he might know whose it was."

Noddy drove to the police station, but Mr. Plod was not there. He drove round the whole of Toy Town, but could not find him anywhere. Fed up, he decided to go back to Uncle Click's and tell Clockwork Clown what had happened. Would you believe it? When Noddy reached the house, Clockwork Clown came out to greet him - with his key in his back. "You can walk!" cried Noddy.

"Yes," chuckled Clockwork Clown. "I've got my key back, look. Where have you been all this time?"

"Looking for that key!" Noddy replied, crossly.

"Mr. Plod brought it round," said the clown. "The Clockwork Train driver handed it in and he knew it was mine. We're giving him lunch to say thank you."

"Oh," said Noddy, thinking what a waste of his morning the whole business had been. He soon cheered up when Clockwork Clown invited him to join them. He had lunch with Clockwork Clown, Uncle Click and Mr. Plod. It was delicious and, in the end, worth spending the morning searching for a lost key!

NODDY AND THE MOON

One night, Noddy was driving home from Big-Ears' house. He normally made sure he was home before dark, as he did not like going through the woods at night, but he and Big-Ears had been having such a nice chat that they didn't realise the time.

"I don't think I shall go through the woods," Noddy thought to himself. "The goblins might be in there. I shall go the pond way. It's longer, but at least I shall feel safe."

As Noddy passed the pond
a duck called out to him:
"Noddy! Come here!
Something funny
has happened!"
Noddy stopped his
car and got out.
He went over to
the pond,
where the
duck was
pointing with her wing at the water.
"Look! The moon has fallen in my pond!" she told him.
Noddy looked. Sure enough, there was the moon shining
up at him out of the pond. What a very peculiar thing!
"What are we to do?" asked the duck. "The moon can't stay
there. How can I swim in a pond with a moon in it?"
Noddy thought. As he thought, the bell on his hat tinkled.
Then he nodded his head and it tinkled again.

"I know what to do," he said. "I'll get a net and catch the moon. Then you can swim safely on the pond again."

"What a good idea!" said the duck. "There's a net in that little shed."

Noddy went over to the shed and fetched the fishing net. Then he put it into the pond and fished and fished for the moon.

He couldn't catch it. He kept thinking he had got it and then, when he lifted his net out of the water, the moon still lay in the pond, shining brightly at him.

"Naughty moon," frowned Noddy, "let me catch you! You can't stay in this pond, the duck doesn't like it, so be good and get into my net."

The moon swam in the pond and would not be caught. Noddy put his hand on his hip with a cross sigh and wondered what to do next. Then came the sound of heavy footsteps behind him, and Noddy looked round. It was Mr. Plod, the Toy Town policeman.

"What do you think you're doing, fishing in the duck pond so late at night?" Mr. Plod asked, sternly. "You should be tucked up in bed, Noddy."

"I'm fishing for the moon, Mr. Plod," Noddy replied. "Look, it has fallen into the pond. This poor duck cannot swim in there when there's a moon in it. See if you can catch it, because I can't."

Mr. Plod began to laugh. He held his sides and roared so loudly
that he startled the poor little duck.

"Ha, ha, ha!"

"Quack, quack, quack!"

"HO, HO, HO!"

"QUACK, QUACK, QUACK!"

Noddy was cross. He did not like people laughing at him and he felt like
throwing the fishing net at Mr. Plod.

"What's the matter, Mr. Plod?" he asked. "Why are you laughing so much?"

"Oh, Noddy, look up at the sky!" chuckled Mr. Plod. "Tell me what you can see."

Noddy looked up and so did the duck. There was the big, round moon floating in the starry sky, shining brightly. It, too, seemed to be laughing at Noddy.

"But there's one in the pond as well!" said Noddy. "I can see it!"

"You look in all the ponds and puddles on your way home," smiled Mr. Plod. "There'll be a moon in every one, but it's not the real moon. It's the moon's reflection. You are funny!"

Noddy and the duck went all over Toy Town together, looking in the ponds and puddles. Would you believe it? A moon shone in every one!

SLEEPY TIME

I've heard my tale tonight,
Now I'll turn out the light,
My hot water bottle's nice
On my toes - they were like ice!
I've had my milky drink,
I'm ready now, I think!
It's sleepy time, I'm yawning,
I shall see you in the morning.

SKY HIGH

Noddy did not realise the moon was in the sky, did he? Look at the things below and first colour in any that you might see in the sky at night. Then colour the things you would see up there during the day. Can you think of anything else you might see in the sky?

WHAT'S THE STORY?

Put these pictures in the right order and tell the story of Gobbo playing a naughty trick on Noddy to steal his car.

A NAUGHTY BREEZE

There once was a goblin called Sly,
Who hid in tree branches up high,
His trick used some bellows
To blow at poor fellows
And make hats fly up to the sky!

WHERE ARE NODDY'S CAKES?

What are those naughty goblins up to now? Noddy and Big-Ears were planning a tea party, but what has happened to their cakes? Gobbo is pretending to be hurt while Sly steals them! Big-Ears will teach Sly a lesson - if he can catch him! See if you can count five cakes, then use your crayons or pens to colour the picture.

NODDY'S LOST BASKET

One windy day, Noddy went out shopping. He shopped until his basket was full.

Suddenly, the wind blew Noddy's hat off! He set down his basket to go after it.

Noddy caught his hat and came back for his shopping basket. It had disappeared!

Mr. Wobbly Man told Noddy that Bumpy Dog had run off with the basket.

Bumpy Dog had gone past Sally Skittle, too. "He went up the hill," she said.

"If you're looking for Bumpy Dog, he went that way," Mr. Jumbo told Noddy.

Noddy was cross as he stomped home. "Bumpy Dog's in trouble!" he grumbled.

Bumpy Dog had taken the shopping to Noddy's house. He was trying to help!

WHICH WAY TO NODDY'S HOUSE?

Bumpy Dog is trying to help Noddy by taking the shopping home for him. Which path should he take to deliver the basket to Noddy's House-For-One?

BUMPY'S BATHTIME

Bumpy Dog, leave me alone!
Why not go and find a bone?
Or get a ball, go out to play,
Oh, Bumpy Dog, just go away!

Tessie's here now - where are you?
Oh, muddy dog, what did you do?
Rolled in a puddle? You're covered in dirt!
A warm, soapy bath really won't hurt.

A BAG OF MIXED SPELLS

Noddy takes his passengers to all sorts of places in Toyland. One day, Miss Pink Cat asked him to take her to Magic Village. On the way, she told him that she wanted to buy a hat from a new shop that had opened there.

Noddy had never been to Magic Village so he felt quite excited. "Here we are," said Miss Pink Cat. Noddy stopped the car to let Miss Pink Cat out, looking around at the little crooked cottages and strange little shops.

While Miss Pink Cat went to get herself a new hat, Noddy looked in some of the shop windows. What funny things he saw! "Hmm, a Spell shop," he said to himself, stopping before a wooden door. "I think I shall go in here."

"Good morning," a friendly wizard greeted Noddy as he went in. "How can I help you?" "I'm not sure," replied Noddy. "Well, if you don't know what you're looking for, the bags of mixed spells are very popular," suggested the wizard.

Noddy thought the mixed spells sounded fun and bought some. He went back to meet Miss Pink Cat, who was wearing a pretty, new hat.

Noddy drove Miss Pink Cat back to Toy Town and told her what he had bought. "You be careful, Noddy," she warned him, before saying goodbye.

Noddy took no notice of Miss Pink Cat. He was so excited about his bag of spells that he decided to go and show Big-Ears. "Hello, Noddy," Big-Ears called when he saw his friend coming up to the house. "It's very nice to see you!"

"Hello, Big-Ears. Look what I've got," said Noddy, going in and emptying his bag on to the table. "It's a bag of mixed spells!" Big-Ears picked up one of the little coloured boxes. "Hmm. Vanishing Spell," he read, and opened it.

A small pill dropped out of the box on to the floor. Big-Ears' cat pounced on it before anyone could stop her. "Whiskers! No!" Big-Ears cried.

It was too late. Whiskers had eaten the pill and WHOOSH! She disappeared in a cloud of white smoke. "My cat!" wailed Big-Ears. "She's gone!"

Big-Ears was very upset. "Look what your silly spells have done, Noddy!" he shouted. "Perhaps one of the others will -" Noddy began. "No more!" Big-Ears interrupted. "They're going on the fire!" "Big-Ears! No!" Noddy cried.

Big-Ears was so cross that he would not listen to Noddy. No sooner had he thrown the last box on the fire than BANG! One of the boxes exploded like a firework. POP! WHIZZ! FIZZLE! "Run, Big-Ears!" shouted Noddy. "Run!"

Noddy and Big-Ears ran to the garden and watched in despair as something terrible happened. Would you believe it? Big-Ears' toadstool house began to melt, just as if it had been made of snow. "Oh, no!" they both wailed.

Soon, all that was left of Big-Ears' house was a sticky puddle. "It's like treacle," Noddy said. "What about my house?" cried Big-Ears, angrily.

Noddy remembered that he had one last spell left. "It's a 'Come Back Spell'," he told Big-Ears. "We shall have to try it, we have nothing else."

Noddy threw the Come Back Spell into the gooey mess and waited. Just as he had hoped, it began to work. "Look, Big-Ears!" he pointed. "The roof of your house is back!" "Where's the rest, though?" asked Big-Ears.

Noddy and Big-Ears watched as the windows and then the door appeared until at last, Big-Ears' toadstool house was back to normal. "Thank goodness!" cried Noddy, running towards it. "Let's see if everything is all right inside!"

Big-Ears' house was exactly as it had been before the spells had melted it. Even his cat was back! "Whiskers!" Big-Ears cried. "I'm glad you're back!" "And I'm glad I have no more spells left," said Noddy. "I shan't play with those again!"

NODDY THE WIZARD

Big-Ears is a little worried that Noddy is going to make
his cat disappear again. "Don't worry, Big-Ears!" Noddy chuckles.
"I don't have any more spells. I'm just dressing up!"
See if you can spot the five differences between the two pictures, then
use your crayons or pens to colour them in.

VANISHING ACT

If you should go to Magic Village
You just might like to stop
At the friendly wizard's place -
He calls it the Spell Shop.

He sells all sorts of magic things
Including magic tricks
But Noddy bought a bag a spells
And got into a fix!

So if you buy some spells yourself,
Beware, and make it clear
That spells are not a food for cats -
Like Whiskers, they'll disappear!

A WALK THOUGH MAGIC VILLAGE

Noddy has never been to Magic Village before.
"What a funny place it is!" he says to Miss Pink Cat.
Can you spot eight funny things in Magic Village that
Noddy would not see in Toy Town?
The answers are at the bottom of the page.

MRS. NOAH GETS A SHOCK

It was feeding time for the animals on the ark. Mrs. Noah fed the cows first.

Mrs. Noah came to the zebras and gasped. One of them was covered with spots!

"Oh, you poor thing," said Mrs. Noah, stroking the zebra. "You've got measles!"

Mrs. Noah fetched a damp sponge. "This will help your fever," she explained.

Mrs. Noah noticed some red patches on the sponge. "How odd!" she frowned.

Mr. Noah saw her. "That's paint!" he laughed. "I'm touching up the stables!"

"Well," said Mrs. Noah. "As you've been so careless, you can clean up this zebra."

Mr. Noah had a better idea. He asked the elephants to do the job for him!

SPOTS AND STRIPES

The zebra in the story was stripy and spotty at the same time, wasn't it?
Look at some of the other animals from Mr. Noah's ark below.
Which ones are stripy? Which ones are spotty? Are there more stripy
animals or spotty ones?

WHAT'S THAT NOISE?

Honks and baas and squeaks and moos,
Clucks and barks and miaows and coos,
Trumpeting and chirruping,
Hissing, snorting, ribbeting,
Quacks and squawks and growls and roars,
Tweets and oinks and neighs and hee-haws,
Above this din, you'll hear, "Dear me!
What a noisy place this ark can be!"

HELLO MRS. NOAH

This is Mrs. Noah. She looks after all the animals in the ark with her husband, Mr. Noah.

Use your crayons or felt-tip pens to colour in this picture of Mrs. Noah at the ark. See if you can match the colours to those on the opposite page.

GOOD OLD BIG-EARS!

Noddy's best friend was Big-Ears, and he often went to have tea with him at his house in Toadstool Wood. He arrived one afternoon with a 'Parp! Parp!' on his car horn, to let Big-Ears know he was there. "Good afternoon, Big-Ears!" he called.

"Hello, Noddy," smiled Big-Ears, opening the door. "Come in and get warm. I hope you're hungry, there are lots of nice things for tea." "Ooh, yes, Big-Ears," Noddy replied. "I'm very hungry. Those cakes look delicious!"

It was very warm in Big-Ears' house, so Noddy took off his hat. He put it on Whiskers' head and giggled. "Don't do that, Noddy," said Big-Ears. "Whiskers doesn't like it and besides, what if she were to run off and lose it?"

"I didn't think of that," said Noddy. He hung his blue hat up beside Big-Ears' red hat, then sat back down to have tea and tell Big-Ears his news.

Later, when the clock struck six, Noddy jumped up. "Goodness, I shall have to hurry," he said. "I promised to pick up Tessie Bear at six o'clock!"

Noddy rushed out of the door, snatching his hat on his way out. "Goodbye, Big-Ears!" he called back. "Thank you for the lovely tea!" Big-Ears ran after him, shouting, "Wait, Noddy! You've got the wrong - ," but Noddy had driven off.

Noddy was in such a hurry, he had taken Big-Ears' hat instead of his own. "What a silly fellow!" sighed Big-Ears. "My hat is far too big for him."

That evening, Big-Ears could not settle. "Noddy can't wear my hat tomorrow," he thought to himself. "If it slips down, he might have an accident."

Big-Ears shut his book. He decided that he should go to Noddy's house and give him his hat, even though it was getting dark. He pulled Noddy's little hat on as far as it would go, then set off through the woods on his bicycle.

Brave Big-Ears thought nothing of riding through the Dark Wood at night. He even whistled a tune, making the bell on Noddy's little hat jingle-jing.

The naughty goblins, Sly and Gobbo, live in the Dark Wood and were not far away. "Listen, Gobbo," said Sly. "I can hear Noddy's bell."

"He must have been to Big-Ears' house for tea," said Gobbo. "We'll teach him to come through here at night! Let's wait behind a tree for him.." The goblins hid and saw a shadow in the darkness. "He's not in his car," whispered Sly.

"Maybe his car broke down," Gobbo whispered back. "Again!" nodded Sly. "He must have borrowed Big-Ears' bike. He'll be easier to catch!"

The goblins put their hands over their mouths so that their giggles could not be heard. They crept from their hiding places and got ready to pounce.

"Get him!" Sly shouted suddenly. Both the goblins leapt upon Big-Ears, knocking him to the ground. They started to wrestle with him, when BIFF! Sly was thrown into the bushes. Then THUD! Gobbo was knocked into a ditch.

Big-Ears got back on to his bicycle and rode off, whistling his tune again and jingling Noddy's hat. Sly gingerly poked his head out of the bush and Gobbo stumbled out of the ditch. "What's got into Noddy?" said Sly.

Big-Ears soon arrived at Noddy's House-For-One and rang the bell. "Big-Ears!" cried Noddy. "You've brought my hat! I didn't dare come back through the Dark Wood after dark. Please come in for a cup of cocoa before you go."

Big-Ears said he would love some cocoa and came inside. The friends gave each other their hats and Big-Ears told Noddy what had happened on the way. "Those silly goblins think you fought them off, Noddy!" he said. How Noddy laughed!

The next day, Noddy saw the goblins in Toy Town. "Hello, goblins!" he called. "How are your bruises today?" Frightened, the goblins ran away. "They won't jump on me again in a hurry!" Noddy smiled. "Good old Big-Ears!"

WHO GOES THERE?

Those silly goblins did not recognise Big-Ears in the dark, did they? You can point to Noddy's shadow, can't you? When you have done that, look at his Toyland friends and draw a line from each one to its matching shadow on the opposite page.

A WOODLAND WALK

Noddy and Big-Ears have been for a long walk in the woods. Now they are ready to go back to Big-Ears' house for some tea and cakes.

DARK WOOD

Gobbo Goblin blocks your path. Miss a turn.

A little duck has got lost. Miss a turn.

You and a friend can race them back if you can find a dice and two counters. Take a counter for each player and put them on the start. Take turns to throw the dice and work your way round the woods, making sure you throw a six to start. In the woods are magic flowers: if you land on a flower, you can go on two spaces. Watch out for goblins, though! The first one to reach the toadstool house for tea and cakes is the winner.

Sly Goblin is following you. Miss a turn.

TOADSTOOL WOOD

NODDY AND THE WOODEN HORSE

Noddy was driving through the Toyland countryside when his car broke down.

Noddy's car often breaks down. "I shall have to push you again," sighed Noddy.

Noddy heard a noise and stopped. "Neigh! Hrrrmph! Help!" snorted a voice.

Noddy followed the sound and found a horse in trouble. "I'm stuck!" she neighed.

Noddy was happy to rescue the horse from the mud. "I'll pull you out!" he said.

Noddy pulled until suddenly, the horse was free and they both fell on to the grass.

"Thank you for helping me," smiled the horse. "Now it's my turn to help you!"

The horse said she would pull Noddy's car to the garage. Noddy was pleased!

A TOW BACK TO TOYLAND

Noddy helped the wooden horse out of the mud, so now she is pulling him and his little car to Mr. Sparks' garage in return. Show them the way to Toy Town without going into any muddy areas - we don't want the horse to get stuck again!